Believe in heroes!

A Fairytale HERO

2024 RAWR ATLANTA EDITION

JANIE CROUCH

Believe in
never!

Copyright © 2023 by Calamittie Jane Publishing

All rights reserved.

No part of this book may be reproduced in any form or by any electronic or mechanical means, including information storage and retrieval systems, without written permission from the author, except for the use of brief quotations in a book review.

This a work of fiction. Names, characters, places, and incidents are the product of the author's imagination or are used fictitiously, and any resemblance to actual persons, living or dead, business establishments, events or locals is entirely coincidental.

Cover created by Deranged Doctor Designs.

A Calamittie Jane Publishing Book

A Fairytale Hero

Chapter 1

Chandra Priestly looked at the Christmas tree sitting next to the cash register and sighed. She'd wanted to do more as the new owner of the Corner Café. Perhaps some lights in the windows, maybe poinsettias on the tables. But she'd just been so buried in everything involved in getting the café set up like she wanted that Christmas décor had been a distant second.

And she really wasn't feeling in the Christmas spirit anyway. Not with her daughter Lilly so far away. So, there was just the artificial tree with a few wrapped empty boxes under it.

Sort of sad, sort of fitting.

She picked up the coffeepot and made the rounds. There were only two occupied tables, and one of them was preparing to leave. She'd already sent home most of the staff. It was time to send home the rest. Why make everyone stay here? She was only open for another hour, and there was no reason not to send Jeff and Sandy home to their families.

She headed for the kitchen and found her closing waitress Sandy with two pieces of pumpkin pie in her hands. "They're finally on dessert. Thank goodness."

Chandra smiled at her. "After you deliver that, go on home." She looked at her cook, Jeff. "You too."

They both stared at her, eyes wide.

"You sure, Boss?" Jeff asked. "I don't mind staying for the last hour."

"No. It's fine. Nobody else will come in. You both have little ones at home—I remember those days of staying up to all hours of the night to make sure Christmas morning would be perfect. I've got stuff handled here. I'll close up after this last table leaves."

Jeff smiled. "Okay. I won't argue with you. The wife's been texting me every fifteen minutes."

She pulled an envelope from her apron pocket for each of her employees "This is for you. Merry Christmas."

Sandy's eyes got wide. "Chandra, you didn't have to do that."

Chandra was still struggling with making ends meet. Starting over at fifty-one by buying this café had been a bit of a gamble. But it brought her back home to Fairytale, where she'd grown up...

The place where she'd actually been happy. She was hoping maybe someday she could be happy here again. After all, the name of the town was Fairytale.

Giving her employees a small Christmas bonus was the least she could do. The last few months had been rough as she'd gotten her feet underneath her, but they'd stuck with her.

"Well, it's not much. But I wanted to do something for you guys."

"Thank you. You're so sweet." Sandy gave her a hug. "Are you sure you don't need help tomorrow? I can come in after the kids open their gifts."

"No. I don't want to see you until the twenty-sixth. Now both of you, get out of here."

"Have you heard from Lilly?"

"She's going to try to call me tomorrow. With the time difference between here and Singapore, it's a little hard."

Sandy touched Chandra's arm. "Tell her we said hello."

Chandra missed Lilly. It'd been just the two of them for so long. But Chandra couldn't let her miss an opportunity to spend a year in Singapore, not when the internship would further her computer science career so much.

Jeff headed for the door. "Merry Christmas."

"Merry Christmas."

Not long after Jeff and Sandy left, the final table paid their bill. Chandra rung them out then carried the dishes to the back. She looked around the empty kitchen. Jeff had done most of the dishes and had cleaned the grill. It wouldn't take her long at all to finish up. Then she could get home.

When she heard the bell on the front door ring she sighed. Maybe she wouldn't be going home so soon after all.

She went into the dining room and found two men at the hostess stand. She hesitated before approaching them, as she tried to shake off the uneasiness they caused. They looked like they'd be more at home in the back room of a bar, or a dark alley somewhere. Anywhere but here in Fairytale. And certainly not in her café.

But she had a business to run. And honestly she couldn't afford to turn away any paying customers, even ones who looked pretty damned sketchy.

She went to them and managed to pull up a polite smile. "Two tonight?"

Why hadn't she just told them the café was closed?

"Yeah, two," the shorter man said.

She sat them at the booth closest to the door. She didn't want them anywhere near the cash register.

"Our cook is almost out of a lot of stuff, sorry. It's a pretty limited menu right now. We've got coffee and he can make you eggs and bacon." They didn't know no one was in the kitchen with her, and she was going to make sure it stayed that way.

"We'll have coffee," the shorter man said. "We're just passing through."

Chandra relaxed slightly as she went to get the coffee. Just passing through...that made sense. A lot of people traveled on Christmas Eve. She'd serve them their coffee and hopefully they'd take off soon.

They were both looking out the front window as she placed their mugs on the table, hardly paying attention to her. That was probably a good thing too.

She did the rest of her closing duties so she could leave as soon as they were gone. When she went in the back she turned on the radio so it would seem like someone was there. She wanted to flip the sign on the entrance to closed but was afraid that might tip the men off that she was here alone.

They finished their coffee and she reluctantly brought the pot back over. "More coffee?"

"No." The man with a shaved head and a scar under his left eye looked around the restaurant, then pulled a photo from his pocket and showed it to her. "You seen this guy?"

Chandra froze, almost burning her hand on the coffee pot as she gripped it without thinking.

The image was grainy and obviously taken without the subject being aware of it. But that was a photo of Jackson Prince.

His family owned half of Fairytale, but she hadn't seen him in years. Decades really. Not since high school. But those blue eyes were kind of unmistakable. That, paired with a head of dark hair, now touched a little with gray, confirmed it in her mind.

But why were these men looking for Jackson Prince? Anybody from around here would know who he was.

She shook her head. "No, I haven't seen him." That was the truth.

The shorter guy studied her for a moment, eyes narrowed. "Word is everyone in town comes here to eat. You sure you don't know him?"

She forced a smile onto her face. "Well, I wish that was true. If everyone in town came in here to eat, I might not be working on Christmas if it was." She took a breath. "But in any case. I don't know this man."

That was pretty much true too...she hadn't seen him in thirty years. She definitely didn't know Jackson Prince in any real way.

The bald guy crossed his arms over his chest. "Maybe I don't believe you."

Shit.

"Do you know who he is?" the short guy asked. "Take another look. Maybe you recognize him."

She didn't want to look. She wanted to figure out how to get them out of here before they realized she was alone.

She backed up a step. "I've only worked here a few months. I don't know everyone in town. But he doesn't look familiar."

She didn't know why she was lying to protect someone she hadn't seen in three decades and who definitely wouldn't do the same for her—probably wouldn't remember her at all.

The bald guy slid toward the end of the booth, face looking harder with each second that passed. "I don't think I believe that either."

She placed the coffee pot out in front of her as if that would ward them off if they tried to attack. "Look, it's Christmas Eve and I'm tired. The cook in the back is ready to go home. I don't know why you're showing me this picture but I don't know this guy."

She almost let out a sob of relief when the bell on the door rang, signaling someone else had entered. She didn't care who it was, as long as she wasn't alone with these two guys. All three of them turned to look at the man—some sort of business guy with dark pants and a collared blue shirt.

He looked at Chandra then at them, with an eyebrow raised. "Still open?"

"Uh, yeah. Limited menu." She was glad to see him so she wasn't alone with these two guys, but still didn't want to serve him anything. She just wanted to go home.

The two guys didn't say anything else, just took out enough money to cover the coffee. Without another word, they walked out of the café.

The guy sat at the bar and shot her a smile. "I'll just have some coffee. I won't keep you on Christmas Eve." He glanced over his shoulder at the door. "Those looked like a couple of shady characters. Are you okay?"

"Yeah, they were looking for someone."

"Well, they looked a little rough. Hope they didn't scare you." He offered her his hand. "I'm Miles. I'm just passing through on my way home for Christmas."

She shook his hand. "Chandra Priestly. Trying to eventually get home for Christmas too."

He gave her another smile as she poured him a cup of coffee. "I'll bet you wouldn't tell those two even if you'd seen the guy, huh?"

She froze. How did he know it had been a man's picture they'd been showing her?

Maybe she was being paranoid, but something wasn't sitting right with her about this man. He didn't look like a thug like the other two, but still...

"Um...No I didn't recognize the photo, so I couldn't help them."

"I see." He looked around the restaurant. "You know

what? I don't want to keep you on Christmas Eve. I'll take my coffee to go."

Yes, please. Just go. She just wanted to get out of here. "Well, if you're sure." She poured a fresh cup of coffee in a to-go cup.

"Yeah." He stood and dropped a five on the table. "Merry Christmas."

"Same to you." She followed him to the door and locked it behind him. She held her breath as she watched him through the window. It wasn't until he got in a car and drove off that she let her breath go. "Okay. A little bit of weirdness there," she said to herself "Definitely time to call it a night." She turned off the lights in the dining room, leaving the Christmas tree lights on, then went to the kitchen. She looked around. It'd take her about an hour to close down properly. She shook her head. "It can wait." She doubted she'd be busy first thing Christmas morning. She was probably the only person in town who had no one to spend it with.

But she wasn't going to let that bother her. She had a lot to be thankful for. The café was finally starting to break even. She didn't have a narcissist husband to worry about any longer. And her daughter was on the adventure of a lifetime in Asia—an internship that would launch her computer programming career.

Not to mention she'd just dodged some sort of bullet with the guys who had come in tonight. Maybe tomorrow she'd call the sheriff's office and tell them what happened. Jackson Prince may not even live here any longer, but someone would be able to get in touch with him and let him know some sketchy people were asking about him.

All in all, spending the holidays alone wasn't too bad.

She turned everything off in the kitchen, then went out the back door to her car. There was room for one car behind the building and she used it. She was the boss. She should have at least one perk.

She got into her older model Honda and buckled her seatbelt before starting the engine. As she glanced over her shoulder to back out of the space, she gasped and slammed on the brakes.

There was someone in her back seat.

Chapter 2

She scrambled for her door handle, but a hand reached over her seat. All she could see was the gun in it. "I'm not going to hurt you. I just need you to drive. Back the car out slowly."

It didn't sound like either of the thugs in the café earlier or even the charming guy, Miles. But somehow the calm, controlled voice seemed familiar.

That didn't mean she wanted to drive this guy anywhere.

She managed to get some words out, but they came out almost in a whisper. "What do you want?"

The man was crouched down, keeping his face hidden in the shadows. "Like I said, I'm not going to hurt you. Just back out slowly." He let out a little grunt with the last word.

She glanced at him in the rearview mirror as he shifted in the back seat. She couldn't stop her gasp when the moonlight shone on his face and illuminated his bright blue eyes.

Maybe it was the picture those men showed her earlier or maybe it was that she'd thought of him way too many times over the past thirty years, but she recognized Jackson Prince right away.

Of all the ways she'd thought of him since the last time

she'd seen him in high school, him holding her at gunpoint had not been one of them.

This night just kept getting weirder.

"You're Jackson Prince." It wasn't the most original thing to say but it was all she could manage.

He scowled. "Please, just drive."

He didn't recognize her. Chandra wasn't surprised. He'd basically been a celebrity back in their high school days—handsome, smart, athletic. Plus, a Prince. That was a royalty in itself in this part of Colorado.

But he still had a gun.

She nodded and backed slowly out of the space, then pulled onto the street. "Where am I driving to?"

"It doesn't matter. Head out of town toward the highway."

Fairytale was like many of the smaller towns in this part of the country—a two-lane road ran through the main section and everything branched off from there. The highway was about five miles south, but even that was a huge Interstate.

She drove in silence, trusting that the man who'd been relatively friendly to her in high school wasn't going to kill her now. Every minute they drove away from town meant less chance of getting help from anyone.

He sat up with a groan once they were out of town. She glanced back in the mirror again. He still had the gun in his hand. It wasn't pointed at her, it was resting on his thigh.

Those blue eyes met hers in the mirror. "What happened to the Stevensons? I thought they owned the café."

Small-talk? Really? She broke their eye-contact. "They wanted to retire and move to Florida. I bought it a few months ago."

"So you moved back to town."

She locked eyes with him again. "You know who I am?"

"Yeah. Chandra Frizzel. I remember you."

It was hard to believe. He'd been three years ahead of her

in school and ran in a whole different crowd. She was the smart, quiet girl whose only accomplishment was being class secretary for three years. There'd only been one time when they'd really connected at all—under the bleachers during a storm his senior year.

"It's Priestly, now."

"Right. Of course you're married."

"Not anymore. I got divorced a while ago."

She'd been wrong. *Now* the night had reached a new level of weirdness. She was having a semi-normal conversation with a man who was basically kidnapping her.

"Sorry to hear that."

"Look, not to be rude, but I don't really want to chat about my marital status or me moving back into town. Not when you're holding me at gunpoint."

He leaned back in the seat and closed his eyes for a moment. "You're right. I'm sorry."

"Why don't I just take you home? We'll call this entire situation a misunderstanding. I'm not looking to press any charges." Not that anyone was going to believe her word against one of the most powerful families in the state.

"I can't go home. There are people after me. That could possibly lead the danger to my family. I've got kids. They're grown, but still…"

Of course he has a family. To think he wouldn't have married and had children was mere wishful thinking on her part.

"What is going on? Why are those guys looking for you?"

He sat up straighter with a wince. "How do you know people are looking for me?"

She brought her eyes back to the road. "Two guys came in to the café. Showed me your picture and asked if I knew or had seen you."

"Shit." He ran his hand through his graying hair. "Did you tell them who I was?"

"No."

"Look, Chandra, I wouldn't blame you if you did. It would certainly be understandable. But if so, we need to turn around. I've got to make sure my family is safe."

She understood that sentiment completely. "I'm telling the truth. The guys were freaking me out a little, so I said I didn't recognize you. I was actually going to put a call in to the sheriff's office tomorrow so they could get word to you that some sketchy guys were asking about you."

"What did they look like?"

"The two with the picture were bald, looked like thugs. One was taller than the other and had a scar under his left eye. They weren't local, that's for sure."

"The Bishop cousins. Brady and Trevor. Was there anybody with them?"

"A third guy named Miles something came in after they left—dressed nicer, seemed pleasant. I wasn't sure if he knew them or not. He wasn't as overt but seemed like he was trying to ascertain if I'd told them the truth about you."

"Miles Tanner. You didn't tell him either? He's much smoother than the Bishops."

"No. Something about him seemed off. He smiled too much."

Jackson let out a humorless chuckle. "Your instincts and his over-the-top smile probably saved my life. The best thing I have going for me in this shitshow of a situation is that they don't know who I am."

He shifted again with a groan. She glanced back in the mirror once more. "Are you okay?"

"I'll live."

"Can you tell me what's going on?"

"I can tell you I'm one of the good guys. Or as much as an

old bastard like me can be, anyway. I've been working undercover over in Harlen County."

Harlen County was a few hours away, but this was at least starting to make sense. "Undercover? Are you a cop?"

"No. One of my sons is sheriff in Fairytale and I was just in a unique position to help law enforcement out. I was supposed to look for any suspicious activity at some of the livestock auctions this week then report back. The situation got a little out of control."

"That sounds ominous. What happened?"

His voice was tight. "I followed some new guys that were making all my internal alarms go off. Turns out my instincts were right. They're part of an insurance scam involving cattle rustling."

"An insurance scam has thugs after you and you hiding in my car with a gun on Christmas Eve?"

He grunted again. "Livestock is a billion-dollar industry. People are definitely willing to get violent to get their piece of the pie or to keep someone quiet about what they're doing."

"I should've done what Beau told me to and reported what I found to him so law enforcement proper could move on it. But I decided to take matters into my own hands. Nearly got me killed. And I'm probably bleeding all over your car. Sorry."

"Wait. What? You're hurt?" Her eyes flew to the mirror again.

"Knife wound in my upper arm. I'll survive."

Crap. This was getting more dire. "Why didn't you go to the hospital?"

"I lost my phone trying to escape from the Bishops and Miles Tanner. I needed to get out of Harlen County so I caught a ride with a trucker. I'm pretty sure they don't know who I am, but it obviously didn't take them long to figure out I headed in this direction."

"I can take you to a hospital now. Doesn't have to be one nearby."

"Hospital isn't necessary. I'll sew it up myself if necessary. I would appreciate if you'd let me use your phone to call my son. I need to report in and see how he wants me to handle the situation."

"Sure." She handed it back to him and he put it on speaker.

"Beau Prince."

That was definitely Jackson's son. His deep voice sounded just like his dad's.

"It's me, Son. I needed to report in. I wanted to let you know that I'm—"

"Dad! Where the heck are you?" Beau's voice sounded completely different than it had when he'd answered a few seconds ago.

"Things went south in—"

Beau cut Jackson off again. "It's Christmas Eve. Can you believe I'm just leaving the office now? I'll bet you're calling because everyone is mad that I'm so late."

She glanced at Jackson in the mirror again. His jaw was granite. "Beau, listen. I need to report—"

"You guys already into the sangria? I can't wait to have some sangria, Dad. Sangria is all I've been thinking about all day."

Jackson paused for a long moment. "Yeah. Sangria. It's what we're all thinking about. See you in a bit."

He disconnected the call.

Chandra shook her head. "I don't understand what just happened in that call."

"Sangria is our family code word when something is wrong. Beau didn't let me get a full sentence in so he's afraid someone is monitoring the call."

"Oh." She couldn't think of anything better to say. This

A Fairytale Hero

whole night felt like she'd fallen down a crime rabbit hole: thugs, guns, carjackings, secret code words.

He ducked as a car passed them going the other way, then sat back up. "It's probably Miles Tanner. He's the Livestock Commission agent I was sent to get info about. He's the one behind the whole cattle rustling scheme."

"Okay, so what should we do now? You need to get your arm looked at and—"

He cut her off. "That's going to have to wait."

"Why?"

"Because that car that just passed us turned around. It's them. They've found us."

Chapter 3

This was an absolute shitshow. Nothing about this day had gone remotely the way he planned, and he certainly hadn't meant to drag Chandra into this danger.

Jackson had hoped the car would simply sit. Or that it was a stranger passing through Fairytale while also *not* being the strangers looking for him. Not Chandra.

He should have known the café had changed ownership. Maybe if he had, he would have chosen differently. *Fuck.* The wound in his arm ached. He needed to get it cleaned and bandaged. But in the choice between being murdered and having a bloody arm, he was choosing the bloody arm.

Glancing at Chandra's face in the mirror, he examined her as lines of worry appeared on her forehead. The Chandra he remembered—the quiet, pretty girl from high school—was long gone. The woman in the driver's seat was still beautiful, but had clearly lived a life. He found himself wanting to know what that life had been and how she'd found herself alone in a café on Christmas Eve. But like she'd pointed out, he had her at gunpoint, and both of them needed to survive if he wanted to ask those questions.

Snow drifted in front of Chandra's headlights. Great. That would definitely help them not get killed. He pressed his mouth into a firm line, trying to keep both his sarcasm and his pain from spilling out. "You know that little valley where we had all the parties back in high school? Pull off there. That'll work."

Chandra's shoulders tightened, and she cleared her throat. "Sorry, you're going to have to be more specific than that. I'm not sure where it is."

"What—"

"I wasn't exactly invited to parties, Jackson." He thought he saw the shadow of a smile tip up before she focused on the road in front of them again. "Too much time spent in the library, remember? I don't know where it is."

He thought some of those parties would have been better if she'd been invited, but he didn't say that. "It's coming up here on the right. A couple of miles. There's no sign. It's just a big split oak. It'll be hard to see, but I'll point it out to you."

"Thanks."

She pushed down on the gas, speeding up. The roads weren't bad *yet*. They had that in their favor, but so did the guys chasing him. At least they wouldn't leave many tracks. By the time the cousins caught up, the quickly falling snow would cover them.

"Here."

They turned off the main highway onto a shadowy dirt road. Jackson smiled. The well-worn tire marks he could see told him this place was still being used as a party location. Some things never changed.

"Should I ask if we're going parking?" Chandra asked.

It took him a second to realize she was teasing him. Referencing…

He'd nearly forgotten the one moment with Chandra that really mattered. Under the bleachers, in the middle of a storm.

Breathless desperation and newness, the taste of the forbidden and feeling like he found something he couldn't have.

Jackson allowed himself a smile. "Haven't done that in a while. I'd be out of practice."

"If I remember correctly, you got more than enough practice for a lifetime back in high school."

A laugh scraped out of him. She wasn't wrong. "Pretty sure I lost it all."

"I hear it's like riding a bike. You always remember."

"Know from experience?"

She laughed softly. "I was about as good at riding bikes as I was at being invited to parties."

They came up on the familiar dead end—a copse of trees butting up to one of the rocky hills that framed the small valley.

"What now?"

"Now, we hide the car."

Jackson groaned getting out of the car. His arm hurt like a bitch. He'd played it down earlier, but it was on fire, feeling more like dead weight than he'd like. The injury wasn't severe enough to make him bleed out, but he knew enough about his own body to know it was dangerous to his arm. He needed to get it managed before too long.

The cold bit into him and his jacket, the temperature dropping swiftly now that the sun was down. Chandra smiled tightly. She was trying to keep the mood light, but there were nerves in her eyes. "If I knew we needed camouflage, I would have driven through some mud on the way to the café today."

He chuckled, tucking his gun into the waistband of his pants as he approached the big pile of broken limbs and branches the kids used to hide their cars when they came here. Exactly like he'd done when he was their age.

Chandra caught on and helped him, and before long the

car was concealed as well as it could be, fading into the background. "What do we do now?"

"Head back to town on foot," he said. "They think we're in a car. They won't be looking for us on foot. If we're lucky, they'll drive right on by, and I'll call one of my sons. We'll get your car tomorrow."

Before she could say anything, headlights shone through the trees.

They weren't lucky.

Jackson swore, grabbing Chandra and turning her into the trees. "Go, quickly."

She did, and he pushed ahead as much as he could while keeping her close. He knew the area, which worked in their favor. But she didn't. So he couldn't just send her ahead and make a stand. He'd dragged her into this mess, and now he had to be the one to get her out of it.

Doors slamming sounded behind them, and he pulled Chandra down the rocky path into the ravine. "Quiet," he told her, trying to keep her calm. One look in the rising moonlight showed her eyes wide with fear. He'd put that there.

Fuck.

Where could they go?

Dizziness washed over him in a wave, causing him to stumble on the rough rocks on the path.

Chandra gasped. "Jackson?"

"I'm all right," he said. "Just some loose stones." Then he let out a chuckle. "You concerned about the man who kidnapped you?"

She made a sound of annoyance. "Seems like you're trying to save my life right now," she said softly, keeping up with him. "And I know you better than that."

"Do you?" He asked. But the sudden lightness in his head made him wonder where the words came from.

"Oh god," Chandra said, pulling his arm too hard. He

barely kept from shouting in pain. "Where did you say you were hurt?"

"My arm."

"That's more than an arm," Chandra hissed. "You've got blood dripping out of your jacket like a leaking faucet."

Voices sounded behind them, and they both momentarily froze. Jackson suddenly forced himself forward, pulling Chandra behind him. The Bishops couldn't find them. They would kill him, and who knows what they'd do to Chandra. Damn it, this wasn't how any of this was supposed to go.

"*There!*" A shout rang out, followed by the harsh, echoing sound of a gunshot. Chandra yelped, and they hurried forward. It was a damn good thing he knew this area like the back of his hand. There was a little alcove where they could hide, and a good thing too. He suddenly felt like he might pass out.

He found the entrance and pulled her around the corner, behind some low bushes before the Bishops had caught up enough to see where they'd gone.

"Here?" Her voice was barely audible, and Jackson slumped against the stone wall, breathless and dizzy. Hell, he wasn't in his twenties anymore. Exhaustion and blood loss were doing a number on him.

Chandra was right, though. This felt like more than it should be. But who knew? He'd barely slept, and the wound had been open far longer than advisable.

Had the knife hit something else? He didn't know. But he did know he didn't have time to worry about it, despite the dizziness and tiredness creeping up. The temperature was also dropping faster and the snow falling harder. Then there were the sounds of the Bishops following, wondering where they went. "It's nearly invisible unless you already know it's there," he whispered.

"And what if they know this area as well as you do?"

"I—"

She had him there. But there wasn't another option.

There was just enough light for him to make her out. She studied him before nodding once. "Be quiet and stay here."

Before Jackson could stop her, she'd slipped out of the tiny alcove, barely moving the branches of their cover. He couldn't even tell her to wait before she was gone—not without endangering her.

Was she leaving to save herself?

One quiet chuckle, and he sank back against the stone. He supposed he deserved that after dragging her into this. On Christmas Eve of all days.

The shuffling sounds came closer. "They were right here. It's not like this place is big enough for them to up and disappear. They've got to be here somewhere."

Jackson's heart pounded in his ears, every beat throbbing with the pain in his arm.

"We'll just check everywhere," the other cousin said. Jackson didn't know them well enough to tell the difference. "If the blood tells us anything, he's not moving quickly."

Flashlights flared around the little ravine, and Jackson fought the urge not to move. If he didn't, there was a chance they'd miss him. He hadn't lied. This little crack in the walls was easy to miss. But they were determined.

Only moving in such slow motion he could barely feel it, Jackson reached behind him for his gun, arm screaming in pain.

They were so close, and they were going to find him. Looking in every crack that existed. He'd hoped he'd get out of this without dying, or without having to kill. But he braced himself—

A blaring sound like an alarm, and a scream, came from the other end of the ravine, back from the way they'd come from.

"Fuck," the man closest to Jackson said. "Over there. *Go*."

Chandra. They found her.

It took every bit of strength he had left to push himself off the wall of rocks and take the steps to get out of the crevice. He couldn't let it happen. He did this. He would help her. No matter what.

Pain stabbed through him as his arm scraped against the rock, and darkness flickered over his vision. This was bad. But it didn't matter. He had to get to Chandra.

Hands landed on his shoulders, startling him, and he nearly fell and took her with him. "Quickly," she hissed. "I used my phone to distract them, but I had to leave it over there. We need to go somewhere, Jackson. Anywhere."

"This way. My family owns a cabin a couple of miles from here. Basically a straight line from the end of the ravine."

The snow fell in thicker flakes and waves, the wind cutting through the both of them and making them shiver.

"Let's go then," she said, sounding more determined than he felt. "Before you pass out. I'm not strong enough to carry you."

Jackson huffed a breathy laugh. "I thought you'd left to save your own skin."

She slipped an arm beneath his shoulder and around him, allowing them to lean on each other as they moved as quickly as they could.

"Don't think I didn't consider it," she muttered. "Couldn't live with your death on my conscience."

"So sure I was going to die?"

She didn't dignify it with a response, and neither did he. Shouts sounded behind them. They'd found the trap and were pissed about it.

Jackson gritted his teeth and tried to stay awake.

Chapter 4

The door burst open, and the two of them stumbled into the dark cabin together, going to the floor. She'd nearly had to drag Jackson the last bit of the way, her limbs shaking with both exertion and the cold.

Her hands shook as she shoved the door closed behind them and locked it. She hadn't dressed for walking miles through snow at a normal pace, let alone half dragging a wounded man.

Jackson was still conscious, but it was a miracle.

The heat in the air took her by surprise. It was warm and a little damp inside—not what she expected for an uninhabited cabin in December.

Fumbling for the light switch, she gasped when the lights came on. A combination of classic and modern, the cabin was *gorgeous.*

Warm, sandy woods graced the kitchen and furniture, with a lovely table, a couch you could sink into, and a king-sized bed that made her want to immediately curl up and go to sleep. There were little decorative touches here and there, but maintained the cool cleanliness of a place that was rented.

But the overwhelming feature of the cabin was the steaming pool in the corner. A natural hot spring, sprawling and taking up at least a third of the space. All the rest of her examinations would have to come later. Because if they didn't get warm, then neither of them was going to be in good shape.

Chandra stripped off her coat and kicked off her shoes, leaning down to do the same for Jackson. He didn't fight her, huddling where he'd stumbled to the floor. Blood ran out of the coat, and it was clearly seeping from beneath his soaked shirt.

She cursed under her breath. That wound needed to be dealt with. But he also needed to be warm. "We need to get you warm," she said, tugging on his uninjured arm and giving him what little was left of her strength. He helped her as much as he could, but said nothing.

Still, when he was sitting on the edge of the stones, he looked at her. Helped her as she got his shirt off and put his gun aside, got his belt open, lifting enough to yank off his sopping jeans.

"In you go," she said, glancing at his wound. She needed to find a first aid kit.

Her clothes hit the ground next to his, down to her underwear, and while she would normally be self-conscious, neither of them had the time to worry about modesty right now.

Jackson groaned against the heat as he slid into the water, and she did the same. It *burned* because she was so cold, but it felt incredible too. This cabin was quite the getaway. She could see stealing away here with someone you loved, spending time in the springs and then moving to the bed.

She glanced over at Jackson, who'd sunk down into the spring, his head resting against the stone with his eyes closed. Neither of them was young anymore, but Jackson Prince was a man who took care of himself. That was clear. She had no idea what his situation was, and it wasn't really the time to be worrying about it, but she could still look.

The warmth was so nice, she never wanted to leave it. But she pushed herself out of the water anyway, shivering slightly, and went to search for towels. A small closet was fully stocked with sheets, blankets, towels, and what looked like some extra clothes. Those would be nice.

Jackson still rested in the pool, with no sign of moving. His chest rose and fell, but he was clearly exhausted. For better or worse, she wasn't getting out of this without him. Wrapping the thick towel solidly around her, she found the real thermostat and got the heat running, and went exploring in the kitchen.

Not much, but she could work with it. She owned a café — if she couldn't come up with something to feed them, she should hang up her hat.

Heating up a little soup took no time at all, and she put on water for some tea while she took a bowl over to the hot spring and a glass of water. "I hope you're not planning to die on me," she said, keeping her tone light.

A smile pulled at Jackson's tired lips. "A little worse for wear, but I don't think the grim reaper is knocking on the cabin door just yet."

"Here." She set the dishes on the edge. "Eat that. I'm going to hunt and see if there's a first aid kit."

Slowly, Jackson turned in the water, a spark of life in his eyes at the sight of the food and water. "It's in the bathroom cabinet."

Right. That made sense.

The food was a miracle. Jackson looked better after a few bites, color coming back into his skin. She left a towel by the springs before going to grab the first aid kit and opening it up on the dining table. It was... impressive. Definitely more than your average first aid kit. It included supplies for stitching a wound.

"Do you normally prepare to be shot?" She asked. "Seems like it."

Jackson chuckled, and Chandra liked the sound. "No, not usually. But this far out of the way, it's better to be safe than sorry. Looks like it worked in our favor this time."

"Yeah."

Water sloshed, and Chandra looked over to find Jackson pushing his way out of the spring, dripping down onto the floor. For several long beats, she couldn't look away from the sight. She couldn't remember the last time she'd been… interested in someone on sight alone. But wow.

His body disappeared behind the towel, and she went back to setting out first aid supplies, fighting her blush. He sat down in the chair next to her. "Thank you, Chandra."

"You're welcome."

"I hate that I have to ask for more of your help, but this needs to be sewn. Do you know how?"

She swallowed. "I've sewn my fair share, but I don't know if it's the same as fabric."

"Similar, but not entirely the same. I'll walk you through it. You'll be okay?"

"I'm a mother. I've seen worse than this. I'll be fine."

He laughed softly again. "Okay."

The kettle began to whistle, and Jackson cleared his throat. Perfect timing. "We can sterilize the needle with both that and alcohol. Can't be too careful."

She nodded and did as he asked, before coming back to sit across from him. "And is there… anything else to it?"

Swallowing, he shook his head. "Hold it closed in one hand and get both sides as close as you can with the stitches. We just need to get it to stop bleeding."

"Is there any alcohol in this cabin?" She didn't mean the rubbing alcohol in the kit.

"I wish."

Nodding once, Chandra took a deep breath. She could do this. Her statement about seeing worse had mostly been bravado. Though she'd treated her fair share of cuts and scrapes, something this deep and ugly had eluded her. "I don't want to hurt you."

"Can't hurt me more than it hurts already," he said gently. "Let's just get through it."

She threaded the thin, curving needle and did her best to push the wound close and ignore Jackson's intake of breath. And keep hold of what little she had in her stomach. One stitch, then two.

"I remember, you know."

"Remember what?" She didn't dare look at him, focused on the stitches as she was.

"That night under the bleachers."

Her face flushed. She recognized that he was trying to distract her from her nerves. It was easy to tell her hands were shaking. "You make it sound much more... illicit than it was."

Jackson chuckled, the sound evaporating as she started the next stitch. But his distraction had worked, because as she continued to sew the wound, she couldn't help but think about that night.

She'd decided to stay late at school to work on homework out on the bleachers. It was a nice day, and it seemed a pity to spend it indoors. So she was studying and the football team was practicing, and all of it had been cut short by a storm coming in so fast, the only way to save her books from getting drenched was to drop under the bleachers and cover them with her jacket.

But Chandra hadn't been the only one to take refuge under the bleachers. For whatever reason, Jackson had as well.

She still remembered her shock when he knew who she was, but she shouldn't have been surprised. Jackson Prince knew everyone.

His smile had been warm and his laugh warmer. With the storm came a sudden chill, and they'd found themselves huddling together in order to keep warmer and drier.

After thirty minutes of easy conversation, it had happened. The rain started to ease, and somehow Jackson's lips had ended up on hers. Her stomach fluttered with the memory. The tenderness and the passion. To this day, she couldn't have said how long they kissed under those metal seats.

Her first kiss, and it had been one to remember.

But at some point she realized she'd been kissing *Jackson Prince*.

"Sorry I ran away," she said softly, trying to focus on the task in front of her. It was almost there.

"I've wanted to apologize for it," he said. "I always thought I freaked you out or took it too far."

"No." Chandra shook her head. "No, it was just my first kiss, and a bit overwhelming, considering it was you. You know, Jackson Prince, star of the football team and everyone's dream guy. I was caught between freaking out that my first kiss had been you, and being grateful you'd looked at me at all."

Jackson graduated a few months later. They'd never spoken much after that. Until now…

"Is it wrong to tell you I still think about it sometimes?" He asked. It had to be Chandra's imagination that his voice sounded rougher than it had a moment ago.

"Only as wrong as me admitting the same thing," she said.

She tied off the last stitch, relieved and unsettled by the dark, jagged lines cutting across his arm. Glancing up, she caught Jackson looking at her with a completely different type of interest.

"All finished."

"I appreciate it."

She smiled. "Well, I can't have you dying on me. I need you to get me out of here."

He laughed and groaned as he stood. "I've never been more grateful we keep the basics here." She watched as he pulled dry clothes out of the closet. They were all big—meant for men as big as all the Prince men were—but they were dry, and that was more important.

"Will this do all right to sleep?" He handed her a t-shirt so large it was sure to swamp her.

"It'll work great."

They changed one at a time in the bathroom, laying out their wet clothes in hopes the warm air would dry them. Chandra didn't think or question the fact that she had no underwear now. The shirt Jackson gave her fell nearly to her knees.

When she emerged, he was standing at the end of the bed with a blanket in his hand. "I think we both need some rest."

"You especially."

But the elephant in the room appeared, nearly visible. There was only one bed in this small cabin. A big bed, but only one all the same.

"I can sleep on the floor," he said. "I'm the one who got you into this mess."

Chandra shook her head. "That's all right. We're both adults, and you and I both know we're too old to be sleeping on the floor."

He chuckled, and the sound went straight through her. Regardless of what had happened tonight, and despite everything, a little spark of excitement went through her at the idea of climbing into a bed with Jackson Prince. Even if it was entirely platonic.

She got under the covers and he took care of the lights, making sure the door was locked and additionally barricaded with a chair. She noticed he brought his gun to the bedside table, and unlike earlier, she was glad he had it.

The mattress dipped as he made himself comfortable.

"Do you know what time it is?" She asked, wondering how much time had passed since her world had turned upside down.

"A little after midnight."

Chandra smiled in the darkness. "Merry Christmas."

Chapter 5

Pulsing pain was the first thing that woke him. Warmth was the second.

When Jackson had fallen asleep, he and Chandra had been on opposite sides of the king-sized bed. Now they were as close as two people could be without being entwined. She was tucked up against his body, snuggling with him like she was made to be there.

He felt stunned. The part that threw him about the last day wasn't the people trying to kill them—that had happened more often than he cared to remember in his life. But Chandra? He hadn't seen her coming.

Their conversation the night before had him strolling down memory lane. It was true, Jackson had thought about Chandra over the years and their single, devastating kiss. He'd even talked to his wife, Lisa, about her a couple of times when they spoke of past adventures. But he'd never questioned why her face stayed with him while so many others hadn't.

Not until now, at least.

With a sigh, he resisted the urge to reach out and touch her further and marveled at the instinct he had to do so. He missed

Lisa. Even after five years, there was a hole in his heart where she had been. An incredible wife, an even better mother. He tried to think of her now as the person she was before the cancer stole all of her energy and independence.

He'd lived a life of twenty-five years with her, and there wasn't a regret in him. His sons had a mother that fought for them until her last breath. Who fought for *him* until her last breath.

In the last five years there hadn't been anyone. A few dates, but nothing more than that. The spark he'd been missing simply wasn't there, and he hadn't been interested.

But Chandra?

She interested him. There was a spark that zinged between them he hadn't felt in years. He was more determined than ever to get them out of this situation unscathed, so he could take her on a date. The image of them waking up together after having a *much* better night wasn't one he could let go of.

Moving with aching slowness, he eased away from Chandra and rose. He held back a groan from the stiffness and pain. God, he hated getting older. Back in his active-duty days in the special forces, a few stitches and lack of sleep would have been like skinning his knee.

At the moment he felt like he'd been hit by a sixteen-wheeler and unceremoniously peeled off the asphalt. Even a few years ago he would have felt better than this.

But pain and stiffness didn't matter. People would still be looking for them—both the good guys *and* the bad guys—and he needed to see where everything stood. Beau was probably losing his mind not knowing where he was. The faster he got to a place with cell service and could get everything handled, the better.

His clothes weren't fully dry, but they were close enough. With his gun once again tucked into his belt, he found the keys to the cabin, removed the chair blockade, and slipped out into the bright morning snow, locking the door behind him.

The sky was clear and the air crisp, the entire world buried under six new inches of white. At first glance it looked peaceful, but Jackson had spent time here. Lisa had joined him on this porch with coffee at dawn more mornings than he could count, no matter the season.

It didn't sound like this.

Silence.

The world was far too quiet.

No immediate signs they weren't alone, but every instinct he had told him they weren't. And no matter what he did, if they weren't, it was now obvious. There was no going back and making the snow look untouched. Thankfully it worked both ways.

It didn't take him long to find the footprints.

Too damn close, and too damn obvious that the cabin had been watched. Behind a copse of trees, and exactly where he would have hidden, was the path of tracks. But where were they now?

He followed where the footprints went, trying to keep his steps as quiet as he could in the snow. At least the sound of snow was softer than normal rocks and branches, the whole world wrapped up in the close quiet of being surrounded by snow.

The tracks circled wide and swung back, almost exactly…

Jackson's stomach dropped. They led directly back to the cabin where Chandra was still sleeping. Whichever of the cousins had found them had played musical chairs with him and took advantage of his absence.

Only his desire to keep the element of surprise kept him from sprinting through the snow, no matter how his body felt. But he moved faster.

Peeking around the last tree he needed to see the door,

Jackson's breath went tight. Brady Bishop stood on the porch, listening at the door with his hand on the knob. It was locked, but that didn't matter. His gun was in the other hand, and he wasn't a man who would have any qualms shooting through a lock.

He only had one chance to take this fucker down.

Bracing himself, Jackson blocked the pain out of his mind and got ready. Not questioning himself, he launched himself from behind the tree, using his momentum to spring over the railing straight toward Brady.

The gun swung toward him, and he tackled the man before the shot could go off. It fired into the air, and a second later Jackson's fist was hitting Brady's face and the gun went flying, lost in the snow.

A punch directly to the ribs had Jackson losing his breath, and Brady got out from underneath him with a hoarse laugh. "Is this really the best you could do to hide? Trevor will be back soon with everyone we need. You got away once, but not again, old man."

Jackson huffed out a breath. It was the truth, but no one was going to call Jackson an old man but *him*.

Brady came at him, the momentum crashing them into the railing. *Fuck* the guy was strong. "After we kill you, maybe we'll have a little fun with her before we kill her, too. You won't be there to protect her after I gut you."

A fist to his stomach had Jackson groaning, but he moved past it, adrenaline, fear, and determination flooding his system. He needed to end this quickly. The longer it took, the more likely that he would tire first.

They traded blows, Jackson ignoring the new bursts of pain in his body, finally getting a hold of Brady and shoving him backward down the steps. He took one breath, then another, both men heaving breath and trying to recover for the next round.

A Fairytale Hero

Brady groaned, rolling over in the snow. Jackson checked any satisfaction the sound gave him, following the man down into the snow. His lungs burned with the cold air, but he could breathe later. Right now he just needed to finish this.

The creaking sound of the door came from behind, and Jackson turned to find Chandra, wide-eyed and blinking into the sun. Nothing on but the oversized shirt she'd worn to sleep. She was caught between being startled and fear, and even in the tension of the moment, he couldn't help but think she was beautiful.

She gasped, and the glint of sun on metal caught his eye. Brady had found his gun in the snow, and it was pointed straight at her.

No.

He moved without thinking, diving onto the man with his entire weight, knocking the gun away from Chandra and wrapping his hands around Brady's throat. The world tinged red, and Jackson moved, raising his hands and twisting Brady Bishop's neck.

Brady's body went limp beneath Jackson, and he blew out a breath, relieved. He took no joy in killing, but this man had not only threatened him and his family, but Chandra, who had nothing to do with this.

Slowing his breathing, he prepared to turn around. Dead bodies weren't easy to deal with on the best of days, and this certainly wasn't that. There was no way to tell how Chandra might react to what he'd done.

But when he stood and turned, she wasn't standing in the doorway. A second later she appeared, with clothes and shoes on, practically scowling as she came out into the snow. She glanced at the body and away, no hysterics to be found. Instead, she looked at him.

"Did you rip the stitches?" She asked.

"What?"

Chandra pointed to his sleeve, covered in blood. "I can't tell if it's fresh or not. Did you rip them? Do we need to sew you up again?"

Struggling in the snow had wet his shirt and made the blood appear fresher than it was. But of all the things hurting right now, his arm was low on the list. He ran a hand over his sleeve. "I didn't rip them."

"Good." She blew out a breath. "Were did you learn to fight like that?"

"Army Special Forces. I was a Ranger." He looked at her absorb the information with a kind of awe. Chandra had no reason to know what he'd done with his life after high school and college. But that little widening of her eyes told him she was impressed, and he liked that.

Clearing his throat, he kept going, reaching down and searching Brady's body until he found what he was looking for. The man's phone. "I trained in a lot of hand-to-hand combat. And other kinds. But killing isn't something I do lightly. Ever."

"I know," she said softly.

"He mentioned that his cousin is coming with others. We can't stay here." Not only that, but the signal out here was spotty at best. Closer to the highway they could use the phone to call Beau and tell him everything.

Chandra smirked. "Fine by me. Let's get the hell back to the car and get out of here."

Chapter 6

The snow started again as they walked. What had been a gorgeous and clear morning devolved into a wintry mess in a matter of ten minutes, the storm blowing through and turning the world to a whirling wall of white. Jackson held Chandra close to make sure they didn't get separated in the snow.

It slowed them down, but they made it to the car before the sun had reached overhead. The car was nearly buried with the snow weighing down what was left of the branches they covered it with.

That was the only good news.

Jackson cursed under his breath. The window of Chandra's car was broken, one look telling him they'd gone the quick and dirty route to render the car stationary. The spark plug was gone.

"I'll make sure to get your window fixed," he said.

Chandra chuckled. "Seems like a broken window is a fair trade for still being alive."

He couldn't argue with that.

"Think my phone's still out there?"

"Probably. But buried under the snow it might not work

anymore. And the cold probably killed the battery." Jackson pulled Brady's phone out of his pocket and checked the signal. Not much, but enough. "Here. We need to call Beau. If there's anyone listening to his phone calls, they'll know my voice. But they won't know yours. I'll help you know what to say."

"Are you sure?"

"You can do it." His fingers brushed hers as he passed her the phone. "Disguise anything directly about where we are, but Beau knows to listen for things out of place."

"Should I tell him it's me?"

"No." He shook his head. "Just act like you know him and that he's expecting your call. He'll catch on."

Jackson moved her away from the car and further into the trees where they had more shelter from the quickly falling snow, and were less visible.

Chandra hit the button and placed the call on speaker. Beau answered after one ring, his voice tinged with desperation. "Hello?"

"*Beau*," Chandra infused her voice with over-polite brightness. "I'm so glad I caught you. I was worried you'd be too busy with Christmas, but you know how things are. Have to check in on one of my favorite people, today of all days."

There was a brief silence before Beau laughed. "You know I always have time for you. We're just finishing up cleaning all the wrapping paper. Have to crunch it up and throw it away before Aunt Sarah gets to ironing it."

Lisa didn't have a sister, but it was a surefire way to tell Jackson Beau knew what was happening. "My buddy still with you?" He asked. "Doing okay?"

"Oh, as good as can be expected. You let him off his leash and he'll get into all kinds of trouble." Her eyes twinkled with amusement as she looked at him. "But he's still breathing, and even the latest trouble wasn't too bad."

Wasn't too bad? He raised an eyebrow at her. Almost

bleeding out, almost getting shot, almost a *lot* of things didn't fall under his umbrella of 'not too bad.'

"Will you be around today? Everyone would love to see you."

Chandra flicked her eyes to Jackson's, and he shook his head. "No," she said. "Headed out of town for the holidays. Needed a little space to breathe."

"Oh? Where'd you'd decide on?"

"Little rental. Incredible place with a natural tub in this hot spring that sinks into your bones. You'd like it."

Beau chuckled again. "I've heard of that place. Sounds like a good place to spend a few days."

"But if everyone wants to see me, I could come home early."

"That's okay," Jackson's son said, almost too quickly. "With this storm rolling in and getting worse, nobody's going anywhere. Pretty much all of Fairytale is grounded. Hell, I'm jealous of you and that tub. Stay there and take advantage of it."

"I will."

"I even heard they have a fireplace there. With a new mantle. Someone told me they made it out of a weird new material. Make sure to check it out for me."

"Will do. From where I'm standing, it's definitely unique."

"Thank you for checking in," Beau said. "I've got to run now, but have a good rest of your Christmas Day and I'll talk to you again as soon as I can."

"Sounds good. Bye, Beau."

She ended the call, and Jackson noticed the way she shivered. "That was amazing. Thank you."

"Guess we have to walk all the way to the cabin?"

"At least we'll already have a trail," he said, putting an arm around her shoulders in an attempt to keep her warmer.

They walked in the soft silence for a while. "So he knows where we are?"

"Yes. I don't know what his plans are, but now that he knows, we'll be in good shape."

Chandra looked to the sky where the clouds darkened and it seemed like the snow fell harder with every passing minute. "It's a good thing you all keep the place stocked with food."

"You know what the Boy Scouts say. Always be prepared."

They fell into a comfortable—if cold—silence the rest of the way back. Both Jackson and Chandra were exhausted, and he was more than relieved at the thought of using the hot springs again, at the same time that he hoped Beau was right and the storm would keep Trevor and his 'reinforcements' grounded for the time being.

He kept Chandra close and listened through the wind, ignoring the aches of his body in order to make sure they were still safe. It was Christmas Day. He hadn't planned on letting them die, but he sure as hell wasn't letting it happen on Christmas Day.

By the time they made it back to the cabin, Brady's body was buried under fresh snow. They were both damp and freezing, and he was grateful they'd left the heat on.

"Get warm," he told Chandra as soon as they were inside and he got the door closed, locked, and barricaded. "Please."

She looked like she might say something against it, glancing at his arm, but decided not to, heading over to the hot springs. Jackson intentionally looked away. The previous night they'd had little choice but to be in the water together to warm up and he'd tried to protect her privacy as much as he could as he studied her face, though he was too much of a man not to notice she'd kept on her underwear.

Chandra groaned as she sank into the heat. "I never thought I needed a tub that was always hot at my beck and call, but I won't lie. This is nice."

"It is. After this, feel free to use it whenever you like. It's the least I can do for dragging you into this mess."

"Sometimes a little excitement is a good thing."

He glanced over and met her eyes as she sank low in the water, that same mischievousness from the phone call shining through. Speaking of the phone call...

"Beau said something about the mantle. And as far as I remember, we haven't actually changed anything about it." He approached the fireplace, noting the supplies there. Neither of them had been awake enough to consider a real fire last night, but after he figured out what the hell his son was going on about, it was at the top of his list.

"I wasn't sure what he meant by that either," Chandra admitted. "But you were right. He caught on very quickly."

"Good thing, too. Hopefully he's right and the storm will slow Trevor and his boys down." He moved all the pictures and knickknacks on the mantle and saw nothing out of the ordinary.

Until...

On the underside of the inner corner, there was a small button he was absolutely sure hadn't been there the last time he visited. He pressed it, and a soft whirring sound had him turning, and then laughing.

A piece of the wall receded to reveal a screen with cameras set up around the perimeter of the cabin. Motion sensors too. It was all running, though muted. Jackson shook his head as he turned up the volume on the alerts. His sons would think of everything.

Though this would have been nice to know about earlier. *Before* Brady had shown up and tried to kill them. Jackson made a note to tell Beau to keep him informed of improvements like this in the future.

"What's that?"

"Security," Jackson told her. "Seems like Beau set up a

whole system for the place." He stripped down to his boxers before joining her in the hot water, reveling in the burn that told him his body was coming back to normal.

"Don't get me wrong, I'm grateful for it now. But doesn't an entire security system for a cabin like this seem a little… overkill?"

He leaned against the rocky side of the springs. "It could be. But we've seen enough things, all of us, that we'd rather be safe than sorry. And like you said. We're grateful for it now."

Jackson was especially grateful. Knowing they'd have at least a little more warning if someone were to come for them allowed the knot between his shoulders to ease just a little. Beau was right.

Glancing toward the windows, he agreed with Beau. No one in their right mind would be out in this storm. Later? Sure. But for the moment, they were as safe as they could be.

Chapter 7

Chandra couldn't remember the last time she was this tired. She worked hard at the café, but between the miles walked, the snow, and all the adrenaline, she was fading fast. The heat of the surrounding water wasn't doing much to help that either.

Shaking herself more awake, she tried not to focus on the fact that Jackson was so close by and that he made her feel things she thought had been long abandoned in her life. She needed a distraction, and she still didn't know nearly enough about his life after Fairytale High.

"Is Beau your only son?" She asked.

A warm, rough laugh tumbled from Jackson's lips. "No. Actually, he's one of ten."

"*Ten?*" Chandra gasped. "How did I not know that? And how?"

His smirk was one more thing she tried to ignore as she pressed herself into the corner of the pool.

"Lisa and I got married in our twenties, and we had three. When her brother and his wife passed, we took in their three. Life came at us and dropped two boys in our lap who needed adopting, and we fell in love with them before we could think twice about it. And then two more additional that aren't Princes, but might as well be. They're part of the family. They're all somewhere in between twenty-five and thirty-five now. I'm a good father, but I'm not keeping track that closely anymore." He chuckled.

Married. He was married. Of course she knew that, but the reality of her thoughts made her blush. She needed to shut anything else down right now. He was saving her life and nothing more.

"Though," he said, "I'm trying to spend more time with them now that their mother is gone. Keep us all together."

Chandra closed her eyes. "I'm sorry for your loss."

"Thank you. Five years ago. Cancer. But we had a good run."

She nodded. "It's not the same at all, but I sympathize with thinking your life would go one way when it actually went another."

"What do you mean?" Jackson frowned at her, watching her almost too closely.

"I got married young, too. I loved him. The plan was for me to work and put him through medical school, then he would work to pay off those loans and I would go to college. It just… it didn't happen like that."

The silence hung in the air, and Chandra realized he was waiting for her to continue. She hadn't meant to derail the conversation with her life's story, but she was already halfway down the path. Might as well keep going.

"After I had Lilly, he decided he didn't want to be a father. That his career took precedence, and he didn't have the time." She tried to disguise the pain of it in her words, but it was something that would always hurt. Chandra wasn't hung up on it. Not anymore. But there was a piece of you that never truly healed when the person you loved most tossed you aside like you were worthless.

"Anyway, I was too busy working to support us to go to college, so it never happened. Like I said, it's not the same."

Jackson looked at her, and a flush rose to her cheeks. The expression on his face was hard to interpret. Somewhere between fury and horror.

"I'm sorry, Chandra. It's hard for me to wrap my head around that. You were always smart. Always had your head in your books." He smiled. "Even under the bleachers. I'm sorry you never got to continue."

"It's okay," she said, making it lighter than she felt. "I didn't need a school to learn. I found other ways."

"I'm sure you did."

Something about the way he said it pulled at her mind, pulled her *closer*, and it was all she could do to stay on her side of the springs.

"How did owning the café happen?" He asked.

Chandra opened her mouth and shut it. There were so many things she could say. Like one of the reasons she came back to Fairytale was thoughts of him. But she wasn't going to admit *just* how often she thought of him over the years. She had already admitted too much while she was stitching him up.

"Lilly is studying in Singapore."

His eyes went wide. "Really?"

She grinned. "Yeah. Computer science. She's having an amazing time. But without her there? City life wasn't for me. Then, when I saw the café go up for sale, it felt kind of like… fate. It's only been a few months. But I'm happy. Fairytale is home. I feel better when I'm here."

The light in Jackson's eyes was intoxicating. He laughed. "Well, I'm glad you're here. I'd be dead if you weren't."

Chandra didn't want to think about that. She floated to the edge of the pool, keeping her body fully under the water. "Now that we're warm, let's see about using some of that food.

I'm sure between the two of us we can come up with something more substantial than soup."

His answering chuckle seemed strained, but in the corner of her eye, she saw him glance toward her as she climbed out before he respectfully looked away. But he had looked first.

She hid a smile.

Pulling a towel around her, she changed into another too-big shirt in the bathroom. They existed in a pleasant silence for a bit while she investigated the cabinets in the small kitchen. Soon enough she heard the splashing sounds of Jackson exiting the water.

Fair was fair. She looked too.

And looked away. She'd seen him last night, and again when he got in the pool. But even Chandra was affected by the sight of him climbing out of water like a perfume commercial. Even if nothing happened between them, she would remember this.

Pulling out options for their food, she startled when he spoke, closer than she realized. "Chandra?"

"Yeah?"

"I'm glad you're back. But I'm also happy to hear you think of Fairytale as your home."

She smiled, because she was too.

Chapter 8

A chirping sound woke him.

Jackson dragged his eyes open and nearly groaned. Chandra was snuggled up next to him again, and if it wasn't the perimeter alarm keeping them alive, he would have thrown something at the damn computer so he didn't have to move from the comfort and warmth of her body next to his.

"What is that?" she asked, waking up, opening her eyes and realizing just how close they were. The day before he'd left her alone. Today there was nothing else to do but to face the gravity that pulled them together in the night.

"It's the alarm," he said. "Get dressed in case we need to go. I'm going to check it out."

Jackson threw on his damp clothes at top speed and shoved his feet into his boots, grabbing his gun. The little cameras on the screen didn't show anyone directly outside, but even if it was just an animal running by the sensor, he needed to check.

The storm had lessened in the night, but snow still swirled in the air as he eased out the door and shut it behind him. He didn't bother to conceal his tracks. If it were an animal it didn't matter, and if it were Trevor and his boys, they already knew he and Chandra were here.

It took no time at all to see multiple sets of human footprints in the snow. Beau was mistaken. The snow didn't stop the ambush after all. And there were too many of them. He felt better after relaxing yesterday and a good meal and night's sleep, but he was still sore, and even in his prime, taking on multiple tangos in a snowstorm would have been a death sentence *alone*.

And he wasn't alone.

They needed to run.

"Chandra?" He burst into the cabin almost too quickly. She was there, dressed and waiting. "We need to go."

She nodded calmly. "Okay. Where?"

No questions and no hesitation. God, there was a reason she'd never left his thoughts all these years. He was half in love with her already, and the trust she showed him was likely to push him the rest of the way.

"Frankly? Anywhere. But we're going to try to get to the highway. Even with the storm, we're more likely to encounter friendlies there."

"Got it."

"I'm sorry," he said, pulling her to the door. "I'm going to get you out of this."

She smiled up at him, and he pretended it was the cold air outside that stole his breath. "I know."

"Let's go."

He locked the door behind them, pointless as it might be, and they ran. Not as fast as they could—they might need that burst of energy later—but fast enough.

It was quiet in the snow, but nothing to tell him they were being watched or tracked. For a brief moment, Jackson thought they would make it clear of the cabin's vicinity without being seen at all. If he could ask the universe for anything—

"*THERE.* They're over there!" A shout came from behind them. So much for pacing their stamina. He pulled Chandra behind him, sprinting through the snow.

Fuck, it was like running on sand.

One glance behind him showed three men chasing. Another glance showed him five. There was no way to outrun them. Not with both of them.

Chandra needed to leave. They needed to separate in order for her to stay alive. And he had to make it so they didn't see it.

Jackson looked around, searching for something…

A thicker grouping of trees was the best he could do. Pulling her into the center, he stopped briefly, chest heaving. "You have to keep going straight. I'm going to lead them west."

"What?" Her eyes went wide. "No."

"Yes."

He glanced out from behind the trees. They weren't in sight at the moment, and it didn't make him feel any better. They were being stalked.

"I can't do this without help, Chandra. And you're the only person who can get it. Now I can keep them occupied, but I need you to go. *Please.*"

She searched his gaze, looking for something. It didn't bother him if she saw he was starting to care too much. That he wanted her safe and away from here.

"Okay."

Turning her, he pointed in the direction they'd been running. "Straight. Go straight in that direction until you run into a creek. It might be frozen, but it's big enough not to miss. It's along the highway. Turn north and go with the creek until you get to the gas station. And call Beau." He tucked Brady's stolen phone into her pocket. "Got it?"

Chandra looked unsure, but she nodded firmly. "Got it."

Taking his gun out of his pants, he held it out to her. "Do you know how to use it?"

She nodded once. "Yes. But you need it."

"You need it more." Jackson pressed the weapon into her hand, making it clear he wasn't taking no for an answer. "Go."

She hesitated for one more second, like something was on her lips. A tiny shake of her head had her changing her mind. "Please don't die."

"I'll do my very best not to."

He watched her go straight into the trees, disappearing into the snow before he stepped out from their hiding spot into full view. Taking a full breath, he shouted into the wind. "All right, you fuckers. You want to do this? Let's do this."

Then he started to run. Away from Chandra.

He lied.

There was almost no chance of him getting out of this alive.

As he ran, he snapped branches on trees and taunted them, pulling them to him until he could hear them following even in the snow.

He might not make it out, but Chandra would. And that was all that mattered now. Jackson had dragged her into this mess, and this was how to get her out.

Chapter 9

Chandra's lungs burned. She wasn't in bad shape, but these last few days had pushed the limits of her strength and endurance. She needed to go to the gym more.

Then again, she hoped she wouldn't be running for her life on a regular basis.

She found the creek Jackson told her about and was heading to the gas station for help. It didn't feel right that they were separated, even though she knew Jackson was trying to protect her. Still, if he was hurt while doing it, was it worth it?

Crack!

The sound echoed through the silence, loud and sharp. No mistaking that sound for anything but what it was: a gunshot.

But Jackson's gun was in her hand.

Terror rolled through her. She was still at least two miles away from getting help, and Jackson could be dying. She couldn't leave him to fight all those people without a weapon. It wasn't who she was.

Chandra turned back. This time she didn't follow the stream directly, instead angling back toward where she'd been when she left Jackson. It would be faster.

Every muscle in her body screamed with the effort, but she ran anyway, worry swirling rampant through every part of her. It was possible she was already too late, and Jackson was bleeding out in the snow. She prayed that wasn't the case.

She hadn't been that far away. The snow was hard to run through, and she wasn't fast. She saw her own footprints from where she'd passed by and slowed. Where would he have gone?

An awareness prickled on her spine a second before solid weight slammed into her. Bright, sharp panic sliced like a knife, though she was too out of breath to scream. But like hell was she going down without a fight.

Chandra kicked and clawed, thrashing in the snow, trying to buck the weight off her and maybe get a hit in too. She was braced for a blow that never came.

It registered a second later that he was speaking. The man who had her. "I'm Beau," he said. "Beau Prince. Please stop fighting."

All the strength went out of her immediately, and he backed away, keeping low to the ground. "Beau Prince."

"That's me," he whispered.

"The sheriff?"

"And Jackson's son."

She blew out a breath. "Don't get me wrong, I'm glad to see you. But do you think tackling me was really necessary?"

The smirk on his face reminded her of his father. "I apologize for that. You looked like a woman on a mission, and I wasn't sure if I called out to you that you wouldn't shoot me."

Grudgingly, she admitted he was right. And the snow had broken their fall, so it barely even felt like she'd been tackled. "Where's the gun?"

Beau held it up. "You mind if I take it?"

"Please. I never wanted it."

She watched as he raised a hand. "My brother Clint is here, too."

"You're here to help?" She asked.

"We're here to do whatever we have to," Beau said, eyes hardening.

Chandra got to her feet, but kept low, following Beau's example. "Jackson's in trouble. Did you hear the shot?"

"Yes." A new voice. She turned to see another man behind her now. But he didn't look at all like Jackson.

She shook her head. "He tried to send me for help, but then I heard the shot…"

"It's okay, Mrs. Priestly," Beau said. "We know he's in trouble and we're here to help. It was you on the phone?"

"Yes."

He smiled. "Thank you for that. And well done. Stay here with Clint. We'll get Dad and be out of this shortly."

Beau was on his feet and moving before she had a chance to protest. Clint took his spot, crouching in the snow and keeping watch. He seemed quieter than the other man. A different energy.

"If you need to go help them it's all right. I'll be fine alone."

Clint shook his head. "All ten of us are here. He'll be all right. Jackson would tan my ass if he knew I left you here alone with people like the Bishops and Miles Tanner on the loose. They'll handle it."

"Oh."

Now that she wasn't moving and her adrenaline was coming down, it was much colder. But she could handle it as long as all of them came back okay. At the same time, her mind was racing and the open silence was wearing on her. "Are you one of Jackson's biological sons?" She finally asked.

"No." Clint smiled for the first time. "I'm one of the honorary ones. You don't even want to know all the shit that happened with my real family, but the Princes took me in when I was fourteen. Last name is James. Legally, at least."

"Well, it's nice to meet you, Clint James."

He shook her outstretched hand. "Pleasure."

Another gunshot rang out, scaring Chandra out of her skin. She leapt all the way to her feet, but Clint didn't seem concerned in the slightest. He looked up at her with mild amusement before he stood to his full height. "Would you like to watch what's going on?"

Chandra blinked. "How?"

Shifting the gun he held, he pulled out his phone and pulled something up before holding it out to her. It was a grid of cameras, all moving together. "Tap on any of them, it'll show you up close."

In one corner, she spotted her face and gasped. Clint tapped his shoulder. "We're all wearing these."

"Why?"

"Same reason law enforcement does. Proof. Accountability. And for reasons like this. So we can see things and go where we need to go and keep tabs on everything."

Chandra nodded, focusing on the cameras, occasionally clicking between the different feeds. They're moving through the woods with ease, and the glimpses she caught of them through each other's cameras showed the same grace of movement Jackson had shown when fighting yesterday. "Were you all in the military?"

"Some of us," Clint said. "But not all. Jackson taught all of us survival and combat here in these woods. We've been working as a team for years. Whoever's out there doesn't stand a chance."

"If they're not too late."

Clint didn't say anything to that.

A sharp whistle sounded from the phone, and Clint looked down. Reaching out, he flicked to the grid and picked up a different video. The screen now showed someone moving slowly. And in front of him was Jackson's gun. They were watching Beau.

On the screen, one bad guy was already down, and she saw one of the brothers take down another one with an arm around the throat. He held on until the man went limp and laid him down in the snow.

A shout drew her eyes to another camera, and a third man went down with no more than a whimper. The Prince boys were ruthless and efficient, tracking down their prey with ease.

Man number four saw them coming, but it wasn't enough. He was unconscious before he had a chance to sound the alarm. That just left one, and Clint shifted the camera back to Beau's.

In front of him, seemingly unaware, was one of the bad guys.

Chandra didn't see Jackson anywhere, but the man who'd been chasing them didn't seem to know where he was. He was moving slow too, ducking behind trees and looking every direction but behind him, assuming there was no one there.

"Here we go," Clint said quietly, backing the phone up to the grid of cameras.

All at once, everyone moved. Loud shouts and yelling, the bad guys being told to get on the ground. There was almost no resistance, and what little there was posed no problem. She felt like she'd nearly missed it because it happened so quickly.

"Woah. That's it?"

Clint laughed. "I wouldn't say that. But I told you. They never stood a chance."

Chandra tapped on Beau's feed again. "Dad?" He called.

"Over here." Jackson's voice was faint on the video. Like the first night when they'd hidden in the ravine, Jackson appeared out of some rocks where it looked like there was nothing. She stifled a gasp. Fresh blood marred his clothes, and she hoped with everything she had it wasn't his.

"Fuck," she heard Beau say. "Are you bleeding?"

"Yup." Jackson's face was hard. "Is she safe? Chandra?"

"She is."

In the corner of her eye, she felt Clint look down at her. What was there to say? The fact that she was the first thing he asked about warmed her up inside in a way she never thought she'd feel again.

"Is it safe to see him?"

"Should be." Clint took his phone back, and they walked further into the woods, meeting the conquering heroes.

The men chasing them had their hands behind their backs, and she had little sympathy for the way they struggled in the snow. She smiled to herself, remembering the phrase Lilly had told her recently. *Fuck around and find out.* If it didn't describe this, what would?

Jackson's arms were slung around Beau's shoulder and one of his other sons. His skin was nearly gray, and he was dragging his feet. But he managed a smile when he saw her. "Told you I wouldn't die."

"You said you were bleeding?"

For a moment, Jackson glared at Clint where he stood beside her, like he was annoyed he'd showed her the feeds. "I'll be all right."

Beau snorted. "Like hell. We need to get him to a hospital. He's torn his stitches, and it's bleeding pretty badly."

"You get everyone?" Clint asked.

"Everyone but Tanner. But my deputies have eyes on him. He'll be picked up soon."

Sirens echoed from the highway as they walked back. Chandra felt a little lost in the midst of all of them. Jackson kept looking for her, but the pallor of his skin was starting to match the snow. She didn't want to be the reason he got any worse.

The ambulance was already waiting, the EMTs bundling him up and onto the stretcher in record time. All she got was a wave before the doors closed behind him.

It was strange, like the sensation of standing on dry land after spending days at sea. Nothing quite fit together and everything felt like it should still be moving. All of it was over. Just like that.

Beau found her as other officers from the sheriff's department and the state police began to arrive. "Will you be all right if Clint takes you home?"

She nodded. "Yeah. I'd like that."

Following him to a car, Chandra stared into the lightly falling snow, wondering how to go back to normal life.

Chapter 10

"Thanks, Beau." Chandra said as she hung up the call on her landline. She needed to get a new cell phone. Hers was still buried in the snow somewhere in the woods.

She didn't know if 'lost it while fleeing from men actively shooting at you,' was covered in the warranty, but she was willing to give it a go.

Beau had called to let her know she needed to make a statement and ask her to stop by the station when she had the time. He offered to help her retrieve her car as well, and get it repaired, which she appreciated.

But the most important thing from the call brought her relief. Jackson was home and resting. Doing well.

He hadn't called her himself, and it was fine.

It was fine.

Did her stomach tie itself in knots at the fact that he hadn't? Yes.

Was her mind racing, wondering if she'd read too much into their connection after all these years? Definitely.

Logically, Chandra knew it was probably something innocent. He'd had to go to the hospital. For all she knew he'd been sleeping since he got back and hadn't had a chance to call her. After everything he'd done to save them, the man deserved some sleep.

Yet deep down, she feared it was more.

Maybe what she'd imagined between them was just politeness and necessity. Two people needing each other to survive and nothing more. Maybe like the kiss they shared under the bleachers all those years ago, it would fade into nothing more than a pleasant memory she would think about sometimes.

The thought made her chest ache, but there was nothing she could do about it. She'd left begging for attention in the past. If a man wanted to do something, he would do it no matter the consequences.

Chandra had learned that the hard way.

At least she'd gotten to talk to Lilly, offer a belated merry Christmas. Chandra hadn't told her daughter any of the details of what had happened—she didn't want Lilly catching the first flight home from Singapore—she'd just mentioned that she'd been busy and definitely hadn't felt lonely.

That had been the truth at least.

Chandra stared out the window now, watching the steam rise from her coffee in the afternoon light. The sun was already fading even though it was early. That's what happened in winter.

A knock at the door startled her.

Hope leapt into her chest. Maybe Jackson hadn't called her because he was coming over in person. She wouldn't say no to seeing him right now. As she walked to the front door, she glanced at herself in the mirror, butterflies fluttering in her stomach.

"I was hoping to hear from you so—"

It wasn't Jackson.

Chandra couldn't place the man in front of her for a heartbeat too long. The café. He came in behind the thugs. He was one of *them*. What was his name?

She grabbed the door and forced it shut, too slow. He caught the door and pushed in through the opening, ripping it from her hands and shoving it roughly closed behind him before locking it.

"Get the hell out of my house."

He grinned, and the expression made her skin crawl. "But I thought you were hoping to hear from me?"

"That wasn't meant for you and you know it."

The man extended his hand. "Miles Tanner. We weren't introduced properly on Christmas Eve."

She didn't take his hand, just staring at him, heart pounding. There was nothing she could do in this situation. The closest things she had to weapons were in the kitchen, and with one look Chandra knew she couldn't outrun this man, let alone out-muscle him.

Miles sighed. "Fine. I hoped we could do this the civilized way, but I guess we'll have to skip over that bit." He pulled out a gun and held it casually. "Let's go have a seat."

Chandra retreated to the breakfast nook where she'd been sitting with her coffee, her heart pounding. What could she do?

Sitting across from her, Miles put the gun on the table and glared at her. "You and your little friend have caused a lot of trouble for me, you know that?"

"I don't even know who you are," she said. "I certainly don't know what you're doing here."

He laughed. "So you're going to pretend you weren't involved in killing my colleagues?"

Chandra scoffed. "You think I killed someone? Seriously?"

"This is getting old." Miles pulled out a cell phone and slid it across the table to her. "Call him. Right now."

"I don't know who you're talking about."

In less than a second, he picked up the gun and pointed it straight at her. The *click* was loud in the quiet of her kitchen. "Call Jackson *fucking* Prince right now. Or your interior decorating is going to get a very violent makeover."

She swallowed. "What do you want me to say?"

"Get him to come over here. And if you give him any kind of hint about trouble, I'll know, and I'll make him listen while I kill you. Got it?"

Chandra's mouth and hands felt numb as she grabbed the phone. "Got it."

She stood to go to the landline and Miles snapped out a hand to catch her arm. "Where are you going?"

"To get the phone number. I don't just keep everyone's phone number in my brain. Enjoy that privilege while you're still young."

He let her go, though she could feel his eyes watching her like she was prey. Her fingers shook as she found the number. Beau had called from their home number today. Quickly, she dialed the number and lifted it to her ear.

"Speaker," Miles mouthed. She put the phone on speaker so he could hear everything. Silently, she prayed this could go as well as the first time she pretended with the Prince family.

It rang a couple of times, and one of his sons answered. Not Beau. Her heart was beating so loudly she missed the name.

"Hi." She cleared her throat. "Can I speak to Jackson, please?"

"He's still resting," the son said. She thought it was Clint but wasn't certain. "But I know he plans to call you later."

Relief flowed through her, and she couldn't even enjoy it. Instead, she laughed like he'd said something funny. "I know. I heard about that. I just need to talk to him for a minute and then I'll let him rest. Promise."

"But—"

"It's a question only for him. If I thought you knew the answer, I'd just talk to you. But you know how it is." Somehow she managed to keep her voice light and breezy. Miles watched her carefully, the gun in his hand, but he didn't look suspicious. *Yet*.

A long silence filled the other end of the line.

"Hello?"

"Sure," he finally said. "Let me get him for you."

She blew out a breath in relief. "Thank you."

A minute later Jackson's voice came on the line, clearly groggy. He *had* been sleeping. "Chandra?"

"Jackson," she put her voice into the light and airy tone she'd used on the phone call with Beau. Clearly fake and over the top. "I was hoping to talk to you."

"I'm sorry I haven't called you yet—"

"I was just calling to see if you wanted to make good on that offer to have a drink with me." She cut him off. "I just made a new batch of sangria, and you said it's your favorite. But you know how it is. It's so much better when it's fresh."

Another silence. "You know what? Sangria sounds amazing. You want to watch a movie? I'll bring over *Holiday Inn*."

"That sounds perfect."

"I'll be right over."

Tension flowed out of her shoulders. "See you soon." Ending the call, she put the phone back on the table. "Satisfied?"

The man smirked. "Jackson Prince likes sangria?"

"What of it? Sangria is delicious. Liking sweet things doesn't make you less manly, or whatever bullshit you've got in your head about it."

"You really want to speak to me that way with a gun aimed at you?"

Chandra sat back down and took a sip of her coffee. "As

you pointed out, it's not the first time a gun has been pointed at me in the last few days. And I think you've already decided what you want to do. So I'm just going to drink my coffee while we wait, okay?"

He chuckled. "I can see why he likes you."

"He doesn't," she snapped. "Wrong place, wrong time. We managed to survive you. That's all."

Miles Tanner looked at her the way a snake might look at a mouse. "Well, keep cooperating and you'll survive me this time too."

She didn't believe him.

JACKSON'S HEAD POUNDED, and everything still hurt. But none of it mattered because Chandra was in trouble. He'd known the second she spoke in that too-bright, happy tone. The word *sangria* was just icing on the cake. He didn't know who was listening, so he'd played along.

"You shouldn't go anywhere, dad."

"And what would you like me to do? Just leave her in trouble? I'm the one who got her into this mess. Like hell am I leaving her to clean it up alone."

Clint sighed. "You're right. But you're barely on your feet."

"I'm fine. Call Beau. Have him meet us there."

"Got it."

Jackson checked his gun before shrugging on his coat and grabbing his keys. More than Clint came with him. Declan, Ezra, and Garrett piled into the car too. Garrett grinned at him. "You didn't think we'd let you have all the fun alone, did you?"

He nodded once. This wasn't something he could joke about, and he was in too much pain to care about levity right now. He broke about a dozen traffic laws on the way to Chandra's house so it was a good thing one of his sons was the mayor. He knew where she was because Clint dropped her off the night before.

Once he'd woken up, he'd planned on calling her and doing exactly what she'd just done. Asking her out on a date. Now he just hoped she was still alive.

They turned onto the block, and he stopped the truck. "Out. If someone's watching, I can't pull up with the four of you."

His sons exited, jogging into hiding places among the trees. They'd make their way around the house and back him up however they could, but this was on him. Deep in his gut, he knew the outcome of this situation was entirely in his hands.

Everything looked normal at the little house on the edge of town. It suited her. Jackson imagined her waking up early and enjoying the dawn in the rocking chair on the small porch, and smiled.

The gun went in the back of his pants beneath his jacket, and he approached the house to ring the doorbell. Footsteps sounded inside, and Chandra opened the door.

For a second, he froze and forgot the danger to them both hadn't ended. Refreshed and in the comfort of her own home, she was beautiful. God, he wished he were here doing this because he'd chosen it and not because his choices threw her in harm's way.

"Jackson," she said. "I'm glad you're here."

Her eyes flickered to her left quickly. And again.

"I wouldn't miss it," he said with a grin. "And I can't wait to taste that sangria you promised me."

She stepped aside to let him in, and he went.

The barrel of the gun came from the left, exactly where she'd looked. It pressed into his temple. "You're a hard man to track down, Mr. Prince."

"I always was good at hide and seek."

He turned slowly to face the man with his hands raised. Miles Tanner stared back at him. Mild shock rolled through Jackson. Beau said he had eyes on Tanner. What happened? If Beau had known Tanner was here, he would have woken Jackson up before Chandra even had a chance.

"You wanted him," Chandra said. "Now you have him. Get the hell out of my house."

Jackson admired the steadiness of her tone and appreciated that she was trying to get him outside where there was room to maneuver.

"Sorry, no can-do."

"You said if I cooperated I'd make it through this," Chandra pointed out, stepping up to Jackson's shoulder. "I've done everything you asked."

"And I thank you for it," Miles said, with his eyes on Jackson. "Now I need you to shut up while I deal with him."

"I will *not* shut up—"

Jackson saw the fury in Tanner's eyes. "I said *shut up*."

He moved, going to hit Chandra, and Jackson moved. His hand slammed into the one with the gun, and pain *exploded* in his shoulder even as his weight took Miles to the ground.

The man was faster than he thought, recovering and grappling with Jackson. But he'd had enough. This man threatened him, threatened his family, and now had threatened Chandra. He would end this.

He drove his knee upward into the man's stomach and rolled them, punching Miles Tanner in the face. Once. Again. And again. The pain in his hand wasn't anything compared to the satisfaction of finally getting to hit the bastard.

Beneath him, the man went limp, but he couldn't quite stop himself from hitting him again.

A hand came down on his shoulder and he shook it off, lunging.

"*Dad*. I think you got him. I can take it from here." Beau

hauled him off Miles Tanner's unconscious body and rolled it over, handcuffing the man.

"You said he was being pulled in yesterday."

"I thought he was. He slipped his tail, and everything we had said he'd left town."

"Jackson," Chandra said.

He took her by the shoulders. "Are you all right?"

"I'm fine, but you're not."

"What?"

Her hands fluttered over his shoulder. All the adrenaline chose that moment to slide into him. "Shit."

The gun had fired into his shoulder, and he was bleeding again. Helping him over to a chair, Chandra smiled. "One of these days I'm going to meet you when you're not bleeding out."

Clint was on the phone, calling the hospital. He better not be calling another ambulance. Jackson was perfectly capable of walking his ass to the emergency room.

"I hope so," he told her. "If you hadn't called, I was going to. The doctor gave me this stuff that knocked me out."

"I thought you might," she said softly. "But I thought maybe it would be another bleachers scenario, too. Something we just think about."

Jackson's stomach twisted. "Is that what you want?"

The smile she gave him sent feelings rushing through his body he hadn't felt in years. "No, that's not what I want."

"Me either," he told her.

Staring at each other for a long moment, the pain slipped back in. "I'll make you a deal," he told her.

"And what's that?"

"I'll get bandaged up, and tomorrow, I'll come here and pick you up for a date. No guns, no blood, and no running. Just some food."

Chandra smirked. "No sangria?"

"Definitely no sangria."

She laughed, eyes sparkling. "Then it's a date."

Epilogue

One Week Later

"I'M JUST SAYING. If I tell you the car's going to be ready on Friday, you can't show up on Wednesday expecting it to be finished and accuse me of bad customer service," Declan growled.

"I suppose it depends on which Friday," Beau said with a grin. "The Friday before? Sure."

Declan rolled his eyes. "You know that's not what I mean, asshole."

"Don't pretend you don't enjoy it when she comes by," Walker said. "I think you like the attention."

Jackson chuckled and sipped his beer. Declan was one of his adopted sons, and Walker was his nephew. But it didn't make a difference. All these men were his sons in every way that mattered. They were there for each other and there for him. Even if that meant helping him change the dressing on his shoulder and managing to get him into a suit for this party.

With a huffed breath, Declan shook his head. "Next thing I

know you'll be suggesting I bring my female clients to our parties."

Walker shrugged. "If it'll make you less grumpy, I'm all for it."

"Speaking of coming to the party," Beau said. "Will Chandra be here soon?"

Jackson nodded. "Should be."

It was New Year's Eve, and the Princes always hosted a party every year. Nearly the entire town of Fairytale showed up on their doorstep, and everyone had a good time. The big house was already crowded with people.

He loved this party, but this year excitement fizzed in his veins. Chandra was coming. Not just as his guest, but as his date. True to his word, he'd taken her out to dinner where there was no danger and no blood, and nothing changed for him. He was interested in her, and for the first time since Lisa passed, Jackson felt like it was a good thing.

Beau put his hand on Jackson's shoulder, like he knew what he was thinking. "All of us saw, dad."

"Saw what?"

A faint smile. "How much she meant to you. Means to you. Clint said you were out of bed and dressed faster than someone telling you there were pancakes for breakfast. And we all know how you feel about pancakes."

Looking between the three men in front of him, Jackson looked for some sign of resistance. Part of his reluctance had always been worry his sons would think he was leaving Lisa behind.

It wasn't the case. It would never be the case. Lisa would always hold a place in his heart. But Jackson was learning his heart was bigger than he imagined.

"She held it together," Clint said, stepping up to their little cluster. "Calm while she watched us come get you when most people would have been hysterical. She was brave."

A Fairytale Hero

"I know," Jackson said. "I—"

"Mom would have liked her," Beau said. "I think they would have been friends if they'd gotten to know each other."

Jackson blew out a breath. "So it doesn't bother you?"

Declan shook his head. "You deserve to be happy. If she makes you happy, then we're happy too. Besides, if she's a secret badass, we want her around."

"Thank you."

Clapping him on his good arm, Walker looked across the party. "You should get over there and stake your claim before someone else has the same idea."

He looked across the party and was immediately grateful he'd put on his best suit and made sure he looked good. Chandra stood in the foyer in a red dress that reminded him of the time they spent in the hot springs. In a good way. He'd had to avoid looking at her curves then, too.

Beau laughed. "Go get her, Dad."

"Hush, boy. I'm working up to it."

Looking at her felt like getting hit by a train. It was the same feeling he used to get when he first met Lisa. Jackson never imagined he could feel like this again, and he needed a second to catch his breath.

Chandra locked eyes with him across the room and smiled. His feet were suddenly moving without him realizing. Hs stood in front of her, still taller even though she wore silver high heels which made her taller.

"You look beautiful." He leaned in to kiss her cheek, the perfume on her skin intoxicating. He didn't want to pull back, but he did.

"Not so bad yourself," Chandra murmured. "Thank you for inviting me."

He held out a hand. "Would you like to dance?"

"Isn't it a little early for dancing?" She laughed.

"Not with you."

Jackson savored the delicate pink blush as she took his hand, not caring at all when people watched him pull her to the empty space they used as a dance floor and held her close. "Hope you don't mind everyone staring," he said.

"It's a little like what I imagine being prom queen was like," she said. "If I'd been anywhere close."

"This is better," he promised.

"How so?"

Smirking, he turned her under his arm. "Well, we're not in high school, so that's a plus."

She laughed. "True."

"Second, we know what it's like to *live*. We know we're mortal, and it makes every moment matter."

More couples joined in the dancing, but Chandra kept looking at him, awe in her gaze. "Yeah."

Jackson danced with her until they were tired, and then he got them both drinks. Then food. He didn't leave her side unless he had to, and people noticed. Let them notice. If he had his way, they'd be seeing a lot more of Chandra and he together.

As midnight approached, he took her hand and pulled her outside. The boys always created this, but they kept it hidden from the party guests in case the family needed a place to retreat. Which meant he and Chandra were entirely alone.

"Oh *wow*," she breathed the words. "This is beautiful."

The entire deck was surrounded with heaters keeping the cold and the snow at bay, with Christmas lights strung overhead in a spangled canopy. The result was a gentle, glowing gazebo just for the two of them.

"I'm glad you like it." He only looked at her.

She looked at him right back. "I do."

Inside, cheers began, and people were counting down from ten. Jackson smiled. "I've seen a lot of new years, but I'm glad to be starting this one with you."

"Think we'll be here next year?" She asked.

"We better be. Cause I'm done only thinking about that kiss. And I don't plan on stopping this time."

Chandra closed her eyes as Jackson leaned in, and his lips met hers as the clock struck midnight. She wrapped her arms around his neck, deepening their kiss, and didn't let go.

He never planned on letting her go again.

•••

THANK you for reading A Fairytale Hero! Ready for more of the Prince family? Josie Jade's PRINCES OF FAIRYTALE, COLORADO series starts with BEAU.

Order it using this QR code:

About the Author (Janie Crouch)

"Passion that leaps right off the page." - Romantic Times Book Reviews

USA Today and Publishers Weekly bestselling author Janie Crouch writes what she loves to read: passionate romantic suspense featuring protective heroes. Her books have won multiple awards, including the Romance Writers of America's coveted Vivian® Award, the National Readers Choice Award, and the Booksellers' Best.

After a lifetime on the East Coast, and a six-year stint in Germany due to her husband's job as support for the U.S. Military, Janie has settled into her dream home in Front Range of the Colorado Rockies.

When she's not listening to the voices in her head—and even when she is—she enjoys engaging in all sorts of crazy adventures (200-mile relay races; Ironman Triathlons, treks to Mt. Everest Base Camp...), traveling, and hanging out with her four kids.

Her favorite quote: "Life is a daring adventure or nothing." ~ Helen Keller.

- facebook.com/janiecrouch
- amazon.com/author/janiecrouch
- instagram.com/janiecrouch
- bookbub.com/authors/janie-crouch

Also by Janie Crouch

All books: https://www.janiecrouch.com/books

OAK CREEK
Hero Unbound
Hero's Flight

ZODIAC TACTICAL
Code Name: ARIES
Code Name: VIRGO
Code Name: LIBRA
Code Name: PISCES
Code Name: OUTLAW
Code Name: GEMINI

NEVER TOO LATE FOR LOVE (with Regan Black)
Heartbreak Key Collection
Ellington Cove Collection
Wyoming Cowboys Collection

RESTING WARRIOR RANCH (with Josie Jade)

Montana Sanctuary

Montana Danger

Montana Desire

Montana Mystery

Montana Storm

Montana Freedom

Montana Silence

Montana Rain

LINEAR TACTICAL (series complete)

Cyclone

Eagle

Shamrock

Angel

Ghost

Shadow

Echo

Phoenix

Baby

Storm

Redwood

Scout

Blaze

Hero Forever

INSTINCT SERIES (series complete)

Primal Instinct

Critical Instinct

Survival Instinct

THE RISK SERIES (series complete)

Calculated Risk

Security Risk

Constant Risk

Risk Everything

OMEGA SECTOR (series complete)

Stealth

Covert

Conceal

Secret

OMEGA SECTOR: CRITICAL RESPONSE & UNDER SIEGE
(series complete)

Special Forces Savior

Fully Committed

Armored Attraction

Man of Action

Overwhelming Force

Battle Tested

Daddy Defender

Protector's Instinct

Cease Fire

Major Crimes

Armed Response

In the Lawman's Protection

Also by Josie Jade

See more info here: www.josiejade.com

RESTING WARRIOR RANCH (with Janie Crouch)

Montana Sanctuary

Montana Danger

Montana Desire

Montana Mystery

Montana Storm

Montana Freedom

Montana Silence

Montana Rain

PRINCES OF FAIRYTALE, CO

Beau

Clint

Declan

Ezra

Garrett

Holden

Locke

Maddox

Sutton

Walker

Acknowledgments

A very special thanks to the *Calamittie Jane Publishing* editing and proofreading team for the Never Too Late for Love books:
Denise Hendrickson
Susan Greenbank
Tesh Elborne
Beverley Findlay
Marilize Roos
Lisa at *Silently Correcting Your Grammar*

Thank you for your ongoing dedication for making these romantic suspense books the best they can be.

And to the creative minds at Deranged Doctor Designs who fashioned all the covers for this series and made the books so beautiful—thank you!